CH00646076

# Pig Surprise

# Pig Surprise

## Ute Krause

Aurum Books for Children
London

First published in U.K. in 1990 by Aurum Books for Children
33 Museum Street, London WC1A 1LD

© 1989 by Ravensburger Buchverlag Otto Maier GmbH
Original German title: *Das Mehrschwein*
All rights reserved
Printed in West Germany

British Library Cataloguing in Publication Data
Krause, Ute
Pig Surprise
1. Title
833'.914 [J]

ISBN 1-85406-058-9

For Nina

Every year, Aunt Agatha phoned Nina before her birthday.

"What would you like most in the world?" she cried.

Nina always knew exactly what she wanted. However, sometimes her aunt, who was a little deaf, didn't understand her too well. So this time Nina was very careful.

"I'll write you a letter," she said.

"What's better?" demanded Aunt Agatha.

"A letter. I'll write you a letter," yelled Nina.

"All right, dear," said Aunt Agatha, and hung up.

Nina sharpened her pencil and got out a piece of paper. Last year, when her dolls had needed new dishes, Aunt Agatha had sent her a bowl with two fishes. And the year before, when Nina had asked for more toys, Aunt Agatha had sent her a tortoise.

Now she wrote carefully:

DER ANT AGATHA
MOR THAN ANITHING i WANT A
GENUIN PIG

YOUR LOVING NICE
NINA

"Something small and soft and furry that I can cuddle," thought Nina. "It would be a nice change after two goldfish and a tortoise."

Nina counted the next few days eagerly. She could hardly wait. Finally, on the morning of her birthday, the doorbell rang.

"My guinea pig!" cried Nina.

Three men lifted a parcel tied with a huge pink ribbon off the van. The parcel began to move. At first it rustled, then it rocked and then, with a loud *craaaack*, it ripped apart!

A pair of friendly eyes peeked out from the wrapping.

A letter floated down from the straw and shreds. Nina picked it up. It said:

> My dearest niece,
>     I searched all over until I finally found Herman. He is a genuine pig and he has the sweetest personality. I hope that you'll be happy with each other.
>     Have a wonderful birthday!
>                               Your Auntie Agatha

"Not again!" sighed Nina.

"That creature shall not enter my house. Remove him at once!" cried Mrs Button, Nina's mother.

But how?

Mr Button had an idea.

He phoned Farmer Hick, whose
farm they visited on school holidays.
"Do you happen to need a pig?"
asked Mr Button.

"Sorry," said Farmer Hick. "The
pigpen is full. We couldn't even
*squeeze* in another one."

Mr Button rang the Macaroni Circus.
"A pig!" cried the circus director. "Can it perform tricks, or count, or do acrobatics?"
"No," said Mr Button, "it's just a plain pig."
The circus director sighed. "Now, if you happened to have an alligator or a tiger..."

Mr Button phoned the zoo.
"A pig?" asked the zookeeper. "If it only had warts and was a nice warthog...!"

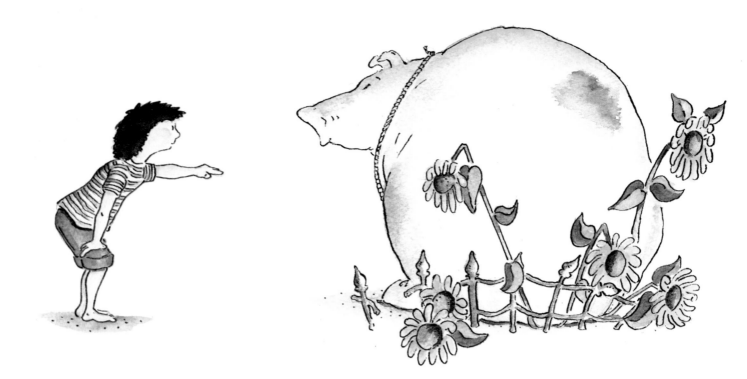

All this time, Herman sat sadly among the sunflowers in the garden.

"He's a rather nice-looking pig," thought Nina. "And it isn't his fault that he isn't a guinea pig."

"Please, Mum," Nina begged, "can't we keep him?"

"My house is not a pigsty," said Mrs Button, holding her nose.

"But—ummm—" said Mr Button. "No one else seems to want him."

"Hooray!" yelled Nina. "Once he's had a bath I'm sure he'll smell much better."

But Herman didn't want a bath. He wanted a puddle.
"And what did Nina mean about my smell?" he
thought. "I smell fine. Just like a pig. No other *pig* has
ever complained about my smell. But Nina is nice. If
only the soap didn't burn my eyes so much."

After the bath, they ate lunch.

"This is much better," thought Herman. He was hungry. The baked potatoes and salad were delicious. So was the gravy. Herman just wished that there was more of everything.

"Herman, NO!" cried Mr Button, as Herman stretched a trotter towards the flowers. Too late.

That afternoon was Nina's birthday party. Everyone played hide-and-seek. Herman loved it. He was always the first one to be found.

"Now let's fish for boats on the pond!" called Nina. Herman's eyes lit up with joy. A puddle. A real puddle! Before they knew it, he was splashing and rolling in the water, squealing with delight.

"Herman, get out of there at once!" commanded Mrs Button.

"Ummm—we must have a serious word with you," said Mr Button. "If you want to stay, you must learn how to behave."

Herman looked at Nina. Yes; he did want to stay.

So they took Herman to the tailor to
be fitted for an extra-large sailor suit.
Herman was proud.

When they walked past puddles,
he shut his eyes tightly.

And, with Nina's help, he even learned
to eat with a knife and fork.

Herman became a model of a well-behaved pig. He learned and learned.

"He's made such an improvement," cooed Aunt Hilda and Uncle Carl when they came to visit. And Herman bowed, just as he had been taught to do.

So Herman was even allowed to go to school. There he learned to sit still, to count up to six and to write the alphabet up to "N" for Nina. Which was rather good for a pig.

Nina and Herman became the best of friends.

They did everything together . . .

even though there were
some things that Herman
found a little strange.

Then, one lovely Sunday afternoon, the Buttons and Herman went for a ride in the country.

Nina didn't care much for these trips. At first, Herman didn't either. But then they passed a muddy pond with some pigs in it. What wonderful smells!

"Pigs!" cried Nina.

"You can smell it," said Mrs Button.

Mr Button drove faster.

Herman wasn't the same after that day. He didn't feel like playing hide-and-seek, or riding his bicycle, or anything else. He spent hours just staring out the window.

"What's bothering you?" Nina asked him.

Herman didn't reply. He watched the clouds go by.

After one week, Nina begged him, "Please. Tell me what's wrong."

Herman looked at her. Then he picked up some crayons and a piece of paper. Very carefully, and a little clumsily, he began to draw. He drew the muddy pond and the pigs.

Nina understood. She was sad, but she also realised that pigs belong with pigs.

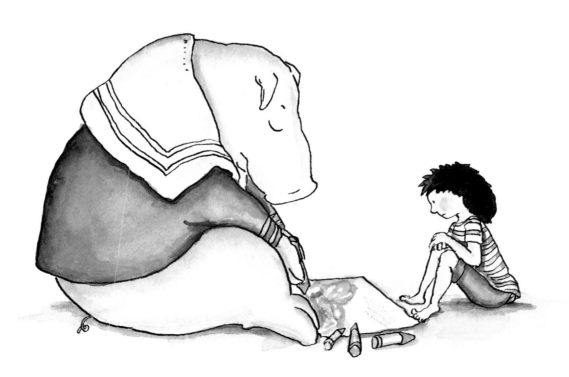

Early the next morning, Nina and Herman walked to the muddy pond. It took them over an hour but they didn't mind.

Herman took off his jacket, folded it neatly and put it on the grass. It made him feel a bit better.

"We're the best friends in the world, aren't we?" Nina asked him.

Herman nodded.

"Will you come to visit?" whispered Nina.

Herman nodded again.

"So will I," promised Nina. "Very, very often."

And that is exactly what happened.

Nina came and so did her parents. They all missed Herman. They had wonderful 'pignics' with Herman and his new friends. But Nina and Herman stayed best friends.